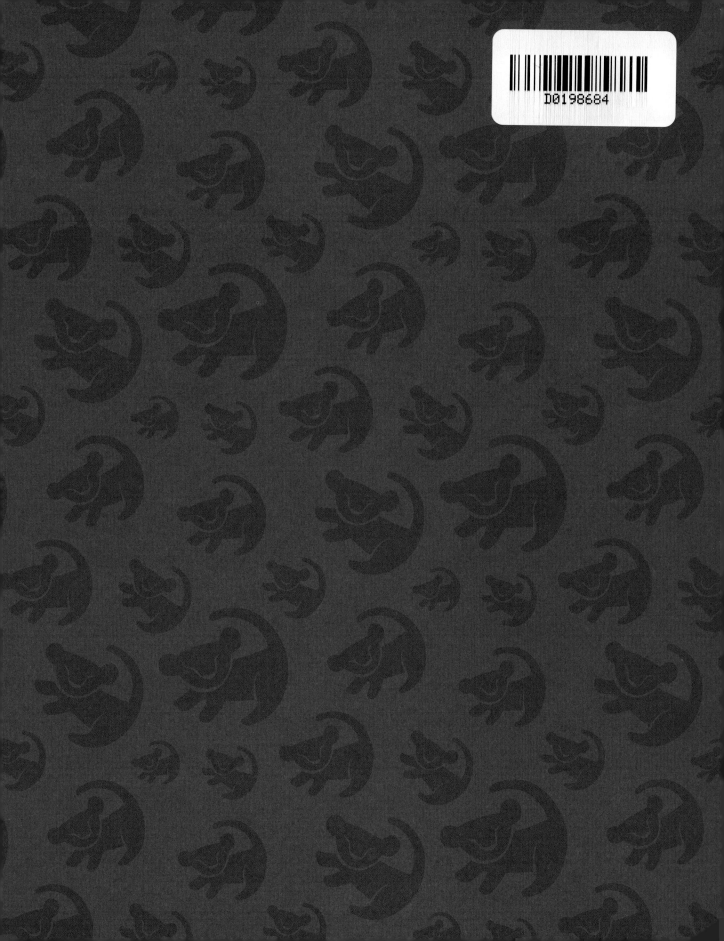

Released in 1994, The Lion King quickly became one of Disney's best-loved films. The story about a kingdom of lions was influenced by Shakespeare's Hamlet and earned a Golden Globe for Best Motion Picture. The story of power, loss and destiny continues to enthral audiences to this day.

Autumn
Publishing

Published in 2019
by Autumn Publishing
Cottage Farm
Sywell
NN6 0BJ
www.igloobooks.com
Autumn is an imprint of Bonnier Books UK

LEO002 0519
2 4 6 8 10 9 7 5 3 1
ISBN 978-1-78905-534-4

Printed and manufactured in China

DISNEY
THE
LION KING

Autumn
Publishing

As the sun rose over the African savannah, a vast herd thundered across the Pride Lands. They were heading towards Pride Rock to celebrate the birth of King Mufasa's son.

Together, King Mufasa and Queen Sarabi stood proudly on the rock as a wise old baboon called Rafiki stepped forwards with a little lion in his arms. Rafiki lifted the tiny lion cub high up in the air and, one by one, all the animals bowed before Simba, the cub who would one day become their king.

Every animal in the kingdom had come to honour Simba – all except one.

Scar, Mufasa's brother, was
jealous that Simba had taken his
place as the next in line to the throne
and did not attend the ceremony. He hid away in
his den but it wasn't long before Mufasa found him.
Mufasa demanded to know why his brother hadn't been
there but Scar just walked away.

"Don't turn your back on me, Scar," growled Mufasa.

"Oh no, Mufasa," Scar snarled. "Perhaps you shouldn't turn your
back on me!"

Time passed quickly and Simba grew into an active, inquisitive cub. One dawn, Mufasa led Simba to the top of Pride Rock.

"Everything the light touches is our kingdom," Mufasa told Simba. "One day, Simba, the sun will set on my time here and will rise with you as the new king."

"What about that shadowy place?" asked Simba, after noticing a dark spot of land.

"That is beyond our borders," Mufasa replied. "You must never go there."

Father and son carried on exploring and Mufasa taught Simba all about their place in the animal kingdom.

"Everything exists together in a delicate balance," Mufasa said. "We are all connected in the great Circle of Life."

Suddenly, Mufasa was alerted to danger in the Pride Lands. He sent Simba home and ran off to protect the kingdom from the hyenas.

At home, Simba saw his uncle, Scar, and told him everything his dad had just taught him.

"My dad just showed me the whole kingdom and I'm gonna rule it all," boasted Simba.

Scar could see how excited Simba was and started to form a plan. Scar slyly asked his nephew if he knew what was beyond the border.

"He said I can't go there," Simba told him.

"He's absolutely right!" Scar replied. "Only the bravest lions go there. An elephant graveyard is no place for a young prince."

As Scar had planned, Simba was immediately intrigued by the idea.

Simba was desperate to explore the elephant graveyard but knew he would never be allowed to go. He made up a story about another place he wanted to see with his best friend, Nala.

"I just heard about this great place! Can Nala and I go?" Simba asked his mother, Sarabi.

The cubs were allowed to go on the condition that Zazu, the king's trusted advisor, went with them.

As Simba and Nala playfully ran through the Pride Lands, Simba secretly told Nala that he had fibbed. As soon as they managed to lose Zazu, Simba planned to go to the elephant graveyard.

After zigzagging through a herd of zebras, the cubs lost
Zazu and carried on with their adventure alone.

As they wandered to the border, they tumbled down a hill
and landed with a thud right next to a huge elephant skull.

Zazu finally caught up with the cubs as evil laughter echoed
from the skull. Three slobbering hyenas emerged from the
darkness and headed straight for the cubs.

Just as the hyenas were about to attack, Mufasa appeared and startled everyone with a deep and mighty roar. He jumped in front of Simba, Nala and Zazu and cornered the hyenas. He slammed the hyenas to the ground with his strong paws and bared his teeth.

"Don't ever come near my son again," he growled.

Simba was safe but Mufasa was not happy with his son's behaviour. He led Simba and Nala home as Scar watched them from the shadows. He was furious that the hyenas had failed to carry out his plan.

By the time Mufasa and Simba returned home, night had fallen on the Pride Lands. Mufasa took Simba to the fields and together they looked at the star-filled sky.

"The great kings of the past look down on us from those stars," Mufasa explained. "So whenever you feel alone, just remember that those kings will always be there to guide you… and so will I."

Scar was angry that his plan to lead Simba to danger had failed and he started to put a new plan in place. The next day, he led Simba to a deep gorge and told him to wait on a rock.

"Your father has a marvellous surprise for you," Scar told Simba.

"Will I like the surprise, Uncle Scar?" Simba asked.

"Simba, it's to die for," Scar promised.

With Simba alone, Scar signalled the hyenas to scare a herd of wildebeests. The herd stampeded down the gorge and straight towards Simba!

Scar pretended to be worried and ran to tell Mufasa and Zazu what had happened.

Mufasa ran to his son who had scrambled up a tree to avoid being trampled on.

"Hold on, Simba!" Mufasa cried.

Using all the strength he possessed, Mufasa jumped down into the gorge and hurried to get his son. He grabbed the scared Simba with his mouth and carried him to safety through the thundering hooves of the wildebeest. But just as he put Simba on a ledge out of harm's way, a wildebeest knocked Mufasa to the ground.

Tired from running through the wildebeests, Mufasa struggled to climb to safety. He hung off the edge of a cliff where Scar was waiting for him. Scar then leaned over him and a sinister smile began to appear.

"Brother, help me," Mufasa pleaded.

Scar dug his claws into Mufasa's front legs and pulled him close.

"Long live the king," Scar whispered.

Then, Scar let go.

As the last wildebeest ran from the dust-filled gorge, Simba saw his father lying still on the ground. He raced to Mufasa's side.

"Dad? Dad, come on," Simba pleaded as he nudged his father.

Simba tried calling out his name, patting him with his paw and pulling his ear, but his father didn't move.

The great king was dead.

Simba sadly settled down by his father's side and closed his eyes. He only opened them when he heard someone calling his name.

"Simba," Scar said as he approached. "What have you done?"

"He tried to save me! It was an accident," Simba said.

"The king is dead! If it weren't for you, he would still be alive!" Scar snarled. "Run away, Simba. Run away and never return!"

Confused and heartbroken, Simba fled. On Scar's orders, the hyenas chased Simba, who leapt off a cliff into a thick patch of thorn bushes below. The hyenas were too cowardly to follow him and agreed he wouldn't survive anyway.

As Scar took his place as king, poor Simba stumbled through the wasteland in the heat of the blazing sun. He didn't know where he was or where he was going but he knew that he could never go home.

Exhausted, Simba collapsed as a flock of vultures circled overhead.

Luckily, a cheeky meerkat named Timon and a kindhearted warthog named Pumbaa found Simba and carried him to a waterhole.

"Where ya from?" Timon asked.

"Who cares?" Simba replied. "I can't go back. I did something terrible."

"Is there anything we can do?" Pumbaa asked.

"Not unless you can change the past," Simba answered.

"You gotta put your past behind you," Timon advised. He gathered a leaf full of bugs for lunch and gave one to Simba. "This is the great life. No rules, no responsibilities and no worries! Hakuna matata!"

Timon and Pumbaa's happy-go-lucky
attitude quickly cheered Simba up.
They taught Simba to live with no
worries and he even learned to
like the taste of bugs!

Soon, he was spending
his time playing in the jungle
and his worries were forgotten.
The days passed and Simba grew
into a strong young lion.

One night, as Simba and his friends lay on their backs gazing at the stars, Simba remembered Mufasa's words.

"Someone once told me that the great kings of the past are up there, watching over us," Simba said.

Timon and Pumbaa laughed.

"Who told you a crazy thing like that?" asked Timon.

Simba laughed with his friends but couldn't shake the sadness that came with the memory of his father.

Wanting to be alone, Simba wandered off. He thought of the past he'd left behind. As he walked, his paw broke a bit of milkweed fluff and it drifted away in the night breeze.

The milkweed flew through the air and reached Rafiki's tree. The old baboon plucked the fluff from the air and studied it. Rafiki could sense there was something special about the milkweed.

"Simba!" the wise baboon exclaimed.

Rafiki realised Mufasa's son was alive and used coloured dust to paint a red mane around a lion cub etched into his tree trunk.

It was time for the true king to return to the Pride Lands.

The next day, Pumbaa was walking through the trees when he caught the attention of a hungry lioness. Pumbaa screamed as the lioness chased him through the jungle.

Timon found the scared warthog just as he got caught under a large tree root. The lioness was about to reach Pumbaa when a loud roar distracted them all.

Suddenly, Simba appeared! The two fought before the lioness finally pinned Simba to the ground. As he looked up into the lioness's eyes, Simba recognised her.

"Nala!" he said. "It's me – Simba."

"Simba?" Nala asked. She too recognised her old friend. "Everyone thought you were dead. But you're alive! And that means you're the king!"

"King?" Timon and Pumbaa asked.

Simba and Nala ran across the grassy fields, chasing each other and playing among the birds. They talked about the things they had missed when they were apart. It wasn't long before Simba started to fall in love with Nala.

Simba wanted to tell her about what had happened with his father, but he was too ashamed.

After his time with Nala, Simba wished to be alone. He was afraid to go back to the Pride Lands and face his past. He was brooding when Rafiki appeared, humming a strange tune.

"Who are you?" Simba asked.

"The question is, who are you?" replied Rafiki.

"I thought I knew," the lion sighed. "Now I'm not so sure."

"Well, I know who you are. You're Mufasa's boy!" said Rafiki.

Rafiki led Simba to a clear pool.

"Your father is alive! I'll show him to you. Look."
But Simba saw only his own face. "Look harder,"
the baboon insisted.

Simba looked again and as he stared at his reflection,
he suddenly saw his father's face staring back at him.

"You see," Rafiki said. "He lives in you."

Suddenly, Mufasa's image appeared in the clouds.
His voice seemed to fill Simba's heart.

"You must take your place in the Circle of Life," Mufasa said.

But Simba was still afraid.

"How can I go back?" he asked.

"Remember who you are," Mufasa said. "You are my son
and the one true king."

As the vision faded, Simba knew he needed to face his past.

The next day, Simba and his friends travelled to the Pride Lands. Simba was horrified by what he saw. The land was bare and parched. Bones lay everywhere. Unlike Mufasa, Scar had not respected the Circle of Life and had allowed the land to go to waste.

As Simba prepared to face Scar, his friends reassured him that they would be by his side.

"We're with you till the end," Timon promised.

Meanwhile, Sarabi stepped forwards to speak with Scar. The lioness had stopped hunting as there was nothing left to eat in the Pride Lands. Sarabi stood before the king with her head held high.

"There is no food," she said. "We must leave Pride Rock."

Scar refused to listen.

"I am the king and I make the rules," he growled.

Furious, Scar lashed out at Sarabi and she fell
to the ground. Suddenly, a deep roar startled Scar.
He whirled around and saw an enormous lion.
Scar's eyes widened with fear.

"Mufasa? No, you're dead," Scar's
voice shook.

"Mufasa?" Sarabi said, but as she
turned around she instantly
recognised the lion as her son.
"Simba? How can that be?"

Scar was determined not
to let his nephew take his
throne. His hyenas began
to approach and they
backed Simba towards
the edge of Pride
Rock.

Scar lunged forwards and Simba stepped back. He lost his footing and slipped off the cliff. As he clung to the edge, Scar leaned over him. Lightning hit the ground and ignited a fire below, surrounding them in flames.

"Now this looks familiar," said Scar as he smiled and leaned forwards. "This is just the way your father looked before he died. I killed Mufasa," he snarled.

Outraged, Simba gathered all his
strength and leapt at Scar.

"Murderer," he roared for all to hear.

The flames burned around them, turning the
sky red as Scar and Simba pounced on each other.
Scar let out an angry roar as he fought to protect
the kingdom he had worked so hard to rule.

But Scar could not defeat Simba, the rightful king. After a fierce battle, Simba hurled Scar off the cliff. As Scar fell towards the burning ground, Simba watched him from the edge.

"Run away, Scar," Simba said, repeating what Scar had told him long before. "Run away and never return!"

Rain began to fall, putting out the flames. Thunder roared above Simba as he climbed to the top of Pride Rock. He raised his head to the sky, remembering his father and all that he had taught him. As the rain continued to wash over him, Simba let out a mighty roar.

The king had returned.

Under Simba's
wise rule, the Pride
Lands flourished
once again. Grass
and trees grew, herds
returned to graze and
food became plentiful.

One morning, as the sun rose over
Pride Rock, Rafiki held up Simba and
Nala's newborn cub for all to see.

The Circle of Life was complete.